For Brian, the love of my life.

THIS LAND
First published in Great Britain in 2024 by:
Bands Together Publishing
www.sarahwoodsauthor.co.uk

A CIP catalogue record for this book is available from the British Library. Paperback ISBN 978-1-3999-8580-2

Illustration and Design by: Happydesigner
www.happydesigner.co.uk

THiS LAND

Written by **Sarah Woods**

Illustrated by **Sarah-Leigh Wills**

The bulldozer stopped and the man stepped out
in front of a woodland that was in his way.

"This land is too full," he said.

Looking down at his feet he saw something wriggling.
"What do you do, you wiggly...

WORM?"

The worm stopped wriggling and said, "My wormholes let in air and water that help the plants to grow."

"I see," said the man, "I suppose you can stay."

On a pile of old logs, he saw something wobbling.
“What do you do, you wandering...

WOODLOUSE?"

The woodlouse stopped wobbling and said, "Munching through this rotten wood, I turn it into soil that feeds the plants."

"I see," said the man, "I suppose you can stay."

On a nearby tree trunk, he saw something flittering.
"What do you do, you mysterious...

MOTH?"

The moth stopped flittering and said, "I pollinate the flowers that bloom at night when bees and butterflies are sleeping."

"I see," said the man, "I suppose you can stay."

Amongst the trees' leaves, he heard a whizzing.
"What do you do, you worrisome...

WASP?"

The wasp stopped whizzing and said, "Bzzzz! I tidy away dead insects and eat the naughty woodland pests."

"I see," said the man, "I suppose you can stay."

Under a pile of damp leaves, he saw something crawling.
"What do you do, you tired...

TOAD?"

The toad stopped crawling and said, "I creep about at night catching the slugs and flies that chew holes in leaves."

"I see," said the man, "I suppose you can stay."

From a branch in the trees, he heard something cooing.
"What do you do, you pesky...

PIGEON?"

The pigeon stopped cooing and said, "I eat the fruits and drop their seeds. Plants can travel because of me."

"I see," said the man, "I suppose you can stay."

In a pile of rubbish, he saw something skittering.
"What do you do, you raggedy...

RAT?"

The rat stopped skittering and said, "I eat the food you waste, and deposit seeds that grow."

"I see," said the man, "I suppose you can stay."

From a hollow in a tree, he heard something scurrying.
What do you do, you scatter-brained...

SQUIRREL?"

The squirrel stopped scurrying and said, "I hide nuts but, if I can't find them, a new tree grows! I've planted lots of trees."

"I see," said the man, "I suppose you can stay."

From high overhead, he heard a cawing.
“What do you do, you crafty…

CROW?"

The crow stopped cawing and said, "I clear the roads of poor creatures squashed flat by fast-moving cars."

"I see," said the man, "I suppose you can stay."

In the undergrowth, he saw something slinking,
"What do you do, you furtive...

FOX?"

The fox stopped slinking and said, "Hello, Man, don't you know? I keep the rats and mice in check."

"I see," said the man. "I suppose you can stay."

In a clearing, he saw something prancing.
"What do you do, you delicate...

DEER?"

The deer stopped prancing and said, "I clear spaces in the undergrowth so sunlight comes in and saplings can grow."

"I see," said the man. "I suppose you can stay."

On the path, in his way, he saw the tallest, broadest, oldest...

OAK TREE.

It was looking down at him.
"Shall I tell you what I do?" asked the tree
and the man nodded.

The oak said...

"I am shelter, I am food, I am a carbon store,
I make the oxygen you breathe and a whole lot more."

The man looked at the tree and all the creatures watching him and said...

"I AM SORRY. NOW I SEE,
THIS LAND NEEDS YOU ALL!"

ACKNOWLEDGEMENTS

I owe a debt of gratitude to so many people. Firstly, thank you to my family for all their encouragement and support. My husband, Brian, our wonderful daughters, Katie and Alice, their brilliant partners, Haydn and Owain and our precious granddaughter, Ottilie. To the many people who have encouraged me along the way, especially Gwyneth Edwards, Deb Henderson, Karen Larvin, Sally Stenton and Sue Weymes, thank you for cheering me on. And, finally, a big thank you to Barry and Sarah at Happydesigner.

ABOUT THE AUTHOR

Sarah Woods is an author of adult and children's books. She lives in North Yorkshire where she enjoys walking with her husband and dog in the rugged countryside. She finds the big skies and expansive landscape have given her a great perspective on life.

ABOUT THE ILLUSTRATOR

Sarah-Leigh Wills aka Happydesigner. Having a child-like imagination and thinking and living in pictures, Sarah-Leigh has a unique way of visualising everything she is commissioned to complete. She enjoys walks and spending time with her fur-family (2 cats & 2 Guinea pigs).